D1246394

MICE *of the* NINE LIVES

TIM DAVIS

Bob Jones University Press, Greenville, South Carolina 29614

Library of Congress Cataloging-in-Publication Data

Davis, Tim, 1957-
    Mice of the Nine Lives / written and illustrated by Tim Davis.
        p. cm.
    Sequel to Mice of the Herring Bone.
    Summary: Two brave mice, Charles and Oliver, help Captain
Tabby search for the Queen's ship, which has been stolen by pirate
sea dogs.
    ISBN 0-89084-755-X
    [1. Pirates—Fiction. 2. Mice—Fiction. 3. Cats—Fiction.
4. Dogs—Fiction.] I. Title.
PZ7.D3179Min   1994   94-26128
[Fic]—dc20   CIP
                                                                        AC

Mice of the Nine Lives

Edited by Morgan Howard

© 1994 Bob Jones University Press
Greenville, South Carolina 29614

ISBN 0-089084-755-X

15   14   13   12   11   10   9   8   7   6   5   4   3   2

Books illustrated by Tim Davis
Pocket Change
Grandpa's Gizmos
The Cranky Blue Crab

Books written and illustrated by Tim Davis
Mice of the Herring Bone
Mice of the Nine Lives

To the kids
of Brown County, Indiana,
who encouraged me
to keep Charles and Oliver afloat

Contents

Chapter One
A Wild Ride

Two mice scurried along the ship's rail. Above them, the wind filled tall white sails. Below them, the waves of the Cattibean Sea crashed against the bow of the *Nine Lives.* Finally Charles and Oliver paused for a rest.

Oliver took a deep breath of the salty air. "Look at those waves." He waved a chubby arm. "They sparkle like the Queen's jewels!"

"Why, my good fellow," said Charles. "You sound more like a sailor every day."

Oliver patted his stomach and sighed. "If only the food were as good as the scenery."

"Well, yes," said Charles. "The bread has been a little stale lately. But Admiral Winchester says we shall soon reach the islands. They are full of delicious surprises."

"True enough," said Oliver. "But not all the surprises out here are of the delicious sort."

Charles laughed.

Oliver wondered whether his friend had forgotten about the pirate sea dogs. Oliver had been thinking about them ever since the *Nine Lives* set out from England.

Finally Oliver said, "I guess you're not worried about pirates. But Mr. Calico told me this morning that we'd be sailing close to San Gato." He shivered. "Now that's an island I'd rather not see again."

"Those sea dogs probably left San Gato long ago." Charles sounded hopeful.

Suddenly, the water beneath them churned with activity. "Dolphins!" the two mice shouted. Soon curious cat-sailors from all over the ship gathered at the rail.

"Let's dive in an' take a swim with 'em!" said a sailor with long whiskers.

"Yea!" cheered the other sailors. "Yahoo!"

"Kin we, Admiral?" called Kitt, a burly sailor.

Admiral Winchester stepped out of his cabin. Oliver thought he looked very tall and grand in his gold-buttoned uniform. "Why not?" asked the Admiral. "As they say, all work and no play makes Jack a dull cat. Ha, ha!"

Several cats dove into the water with the frisky dolphins. The Admiral and the first mate, Mr. Calico, joined Charles and Oliver at the rail to watch the fun.

Many of the sailors grabbed onto a fin and took a ride. But the dolphins were slippery, and it was hard to stay on their backs.

"Ha, look at those chaps! What a ride!" said Charles.

"They can't even stay on!" Oliver said with a laugh. "Admiral, may I borrow your scope?"

Admiral Winchester kept a small telescope hooked onto his belt with a loop of string. He smiled and handed it down to his friend. Oliver stood on the rail, holding the scope in both hands. He peered through it and began laughing again. He laughed so hard it was hard for him to see.

"You should have seen that Kitt's face—" he said, giggling. "—Trying so hard to hold onto that slippery fish!" He bent over with laughter and lost his balance. His feet slipped out from underneath him. "Whoooooa!"

Splash! He fell into the water, still holding the scope. Suddenly he was bounced back out of the water by a dolphin's snout. He did a flip in midair and landed on the dolphin's back. Before he could catch his breath, he began slipping and skidding along the dolphin's back.

He hit the dolphin's fin, and the string on the telescope hooked around the fin. Oliver clamped his fingers onto the end of the scope and held on for dear life. The scope slid out to its full length, and he found himself being pulled through the water at full speed.

"Help!" he cried. A dolphin-riding sailor splashed over and snatched him up.

Oliver gulped down a mouthful of seawater and sneezed a couple of times. "Thanks, Kitt," he gasped.

"What 'er friends for, mate?" Kitt tossed the telescope back up to the ship. "Here ye go, Admiral."

The Admiral fumbled at the scope and almost dropped it. Mr. Calico snatched it out of the air, dried it on his shirt, and handed it to him.

"How's the water?" shouted Charles. He grinned down at Oliver.

"A mite more slippery than I figured," Oliver called back.

Charles laughed, then he turned to the Admiral. "I'm tempted to borrow your scope just to see how red Oliver's face is about now."

"Go ahead, my good mouse. As they say, he who laughs first, laughs worst." The Admiral handed the scope to Charles.

Charles lifted the scope to his eyes. Mr. Calico gripped the mouse's tail, just in case, and Charles stopped laughing.

"Why, Charles," said the first mate. "What do you see?"

"It's a ship—no—just a small skiff." Charles frowned and squinted into the scope again. "It's overloaded with crew. Looks like they're signaling for help!"

Chapter Two
To the Rescue

Oliver and the cats climbed back onboard immediately. The *Nine Lives* steered toward the little skiff, speeding to the rescue.

As they got closer, Charles exclaimed, "Looks like more of the Queen's cats."

Oliver sighed. "At least they're not sea dogs."

Mr. Calico nodded. "But why would they sail with just a flag. . . ."

"My dear Mr. Calico," said Admiral Winchester. "The flag of our country and our Queen is not just a flag! It is the glorious symbol of our mighty union!"

"I beg your pardon, sir," said Mr. Calico. "But I meant to point out that they have no ordinary sail, and they're far out to sea. That does not seem like a good idea."

The Admiral puffed out his chest and cleared his throat. "Yes, of course, Mr. Calico."

Soon the *Nine Lives* pulled close to the skiff. The crew threw ropes down and the new passengers quickly climbed onboard. They put their little boat in tow.

Oliver noticed how lean and hungry these cats looked. He leaned over and whispered to Charles, "Perhaps we should stay out of sight until they've had a bite to eat." He slipped behind Mr. Calico, just in case.

To his relief, a tall, striped cat exclaimed, "Winchester and Calico! My good friends!

How good to see you, and at such a time!"

"Well, could this be Captain Tabby?" asked the Admiral. Soon they were all smiling and shaking hands. Food and water were brought to the hungry cats, and the crews were introduced to each other. Then Admiral Winchester introduced the mice: "And formerly of the *Herring Bone,* my two brave mouse friends, Charles—"

Charles bowed.

"And Ol—uh—where is Oliver?" said the Admiral. Oliver peeked out from behind Mr. Calico's boot.

Captain Tabby chuckled. "Good to meet you, my fine mice!" He bowed too. "I have heard of your—ahem—brave deeds in the service of our Queen."

"My dear Tabby, do tell us how you came to be here," said the Admiral. "And how does it happen that you are in such a state of need?"

The tall striped cat began his tale. "We were sailing in the service of the Queen—on the great ship the *Seven Seas*. First we were blown off course in a gale, then we had to pass through the Straits of San Desperado. Remember those terrible jagged rocks? That is where we were ambushed by pirates."

Oliver gasped.

The Captain nodded at him. "They used vines to swing down from the rocks. Suddenly the ship was filled with pirate sea dogs. Before we could move to defend ourselves, they had taken over the ship. We were their prisoners. Then they sailed the *Seven Seas* far out into the Cattibean Sea.

"There, in the middle of nowhere, the pirates set us adrift in our skiff. They refused us a sail. They gave us only our flag."

"Such a common use of so great a banner!" said Mr. Calico. Admiral Winchester nodded his agreement.

"Then a curious thing happened," said Captain Tabby. "Those sea dogs hoisted a flag of their own on the mast of the *Seven Seas.* But 'twasn't the skull and crossbones so oft used by those sort of rebels. Instead, it displayed the bones of a fish!"

"You don't say." The Admiral raised an eyebrow. "And those fish bones, they wouldn't have looked like a herring, now would they?"

"The *Herring Bone!*" said Captain Tabby. "Of course, that was it."

"Oh, no!" moaned Oliver.

Charles shook his head. "Oliver, I'm afraid the very worst of your fears may be true after all. We must come face to face with the terrible Captain Crag and his crew of mangy sea dogs yet again."

Chapter Three
Kept at Bay

All the cats agreed that it was only their proper duty. They must do everything possible to find the *Seven Seas* and bring it back into the Queen's service. But where had the pirates taken the grand ship?

Admiral Winchester, Mr. Calico, Captain Tabby, and the two mice shut themselves into the Admiral's cabin. The Admiral pulled out a big scroll of paper and unrolled it on the table. It was a map of the Cattibean Sea. Charles and Oliver stood on the map, studying the islands, inlets, and other mysterious-looking places.

Charles sighed. "How will we ever find a ship full of pirates in this maze of islands?"

"Perhaps we won't," said Oliver.

"Actually, it may not be as hard as you think," said Captain Tabby. "This is where we are now." He made a chalk mark on the map. "If we go southeast—like this—we will be about here." He marked another spot. "That's about where the *Seven Seas* would have been when we were set adrift."

Then the Captain drew again with his chalk. He made a circle around the area where the two mice were standing. "They've got to be somewhere in this circle."

Charles looked closely at the map. "Looks like here's a nice bay for a big ship." He pointed to an island right under Oliver's feet.

CATTIBEAN SEA

TROPICK OF CANCER

PAIRAQUETO

FELINO

PAJAMA

FIDELO

FLORATAN

TERRA FIRMA

TOICAN

MAÑANA

N E S W

"San FY-ee-RO?" asked Oliver, reading the type by his toes.

"Pronounced Fee-AIR-oh, my good mouse," the Admiral said.

"You know of the island?" asked the Captain.

"Aye, 'tis lonely and mountainous, and it has an active volcano," said the Admiral. Oliver stepped off the island and backed up a few steps. "And our friend Charles is quite right," the Admiral added. "It's a good place to anchor a big ship."

So they set off in search of San Fiero and the *Seven Seas*. After two days of sailing, they came upon the island at dawn. It was a strangely dark morning, Oliver thought. It seemed hazy. Or was it smoky?

"Hard to see in this haze, eh, Mr. Calico?" said Admiral Winchester.

Mr. Calico nodded. "Aye, sir, that it is."

"That may work to our advantage," said Charles.

The two cats looked surprised.

"If the pirates are here," said Charles, "we should be safely into the island's bay before they see us coming."

"You're right!" said the Admiral. "We could keep them at bay, as it were, couldn't we?"

"Precisely," said Charles. "They could never escape to the sea. The entrance to the bay is too narrow."

"Good show!" exclaimed Mr. Calico.

"Thank you," the Admiral said.

Mr. Calico looked at Charles, but Charles only winked at him. Then he winked at Oliver.

"Most welcome, sir," added Mr. Calico.

So the *Nine Lives* sailed closer, and the hazy smoke grew thicker. As planned, Mr. Calico kept the ship in the darkest section of the haze. Then he steered sharply toward the bay's narrow entrance. Here the smoke lifted a little. Through the haze loomed the dark shape of a ship—a big ship anchored in the bay. Yes, Oliver thought, it's the *Seven Seas!*

"Eureka!" cried the Admiral. Captain Tabby grinned up at the great ship.

"Steer her in carefully, Mr. Calico," said the Admiral. "We'll anchor the *Nine Lives* just inside the bay but out of cannon range."

"Aye, aye, sir."

23

A shiver went up Oliver's spine. It wasn't the coolness of the morning air. It was the sight of that flag again—the banner of the *Herring Bone.*

At the Admiral's command, Mr. Calico rang the ship's bell. Admiral Winchester puffed out his chest and cleared his throat. "Attention! Attention! Surrender your ship! I command you by the authority of the Queen of England, surrender immediately!"

They heard a sudden hustling and bustling aboard the pirate ship. Surely the sea dogs had been caught by surprise! Oliver held his breath.

At last a familiar voice boomed across the water. "An' what if'n we refuse, ye flea-bitten hairballs?"

No doubt about it, that was Captain Crag!

"Escape is impossible!" said Admiral Winchester. "Surrender or the *Seven Seas* shall be taken back by force!"

Oliver glanced at Charles. "I wish he hadn't said that! Nobody loves a fight like Crag."

"Maybe so," said Charles. "But we've caught him napping, as it were, and cornered too."

They heard a great deal of mumbling and grumbling across the water.

Finally, Crag called back. "Admril, ye got us plugged in 'ere like a ship in a bottle. Ye knows its ag'inst me nature, but we surrender—"

Oliver could hardly believe his ears.

"—on one condition."

Charles shook his head.

"Admril," said Crag, "I want ye ta come out here in yer skiff and meet me, one ta one. We kin discuss the terms of the surrender."

Before anyone could stop him, Admiral Winchester shouted back. "Agreed!" He started for the skiff.

"But Admiral—" said Mr. Calico.

"You can't trust that scoundrel," Charles said. "It could be a trap! At least let us sneak along with you in secret."

Oliver stared at Charles, wide-eyed.

"I'm sorry, my good mice," said the Admiral. "But I've given my word, and I'll go it alone." He drew himself up to his full height. "It's the only honorable thing to do!"

He lowered the skiff and rowed through the haze toward the *Seven Seas*.

Chapter Four
An Admiral's Ransom

The entire crew, including Captain Tabby and his cats, stood at the rail of the *Nine Lives*. Oliver strained to see what was happening through the haze. Nervously, he glanced around. It looked like no one else could see.

"I have an uneasy feeling about this arrangement," said Charles. "I wish the Admiral had let us come along."

"Once he gave his word, I knew there'd be no changing his mind." Mr. Calico sighed.

Oliver could just barely see the shapes of the two skiffs. They seemed to be about halfway between the *Nine Lives* and the *Seven Seas.* The Admiral sat alone in his skiff, with Crag alongside in his. But was Crag alone or not? It was hard to tell in the haze. Oliver could hear muffled voices. Sounded like an argument out there. He strained his ears, but still he could not tell what was happening.

Suddenly the voices stopped. Then both skiffs faded into the haze.

"Looks like they're going back to the *Seven Seas!*" Charles squeaked.

"Why would they do that?" asked Oliver.

"Doesn't seem right to me," said Mr. Calico. "Prepare to close in, mates!"

The cats rushed around the ship. They refurled the sails and lifted the anchor. The *Nine Lives* groaned and creaked and moved farther into the harbor. Soon the *Seven Seas* was within the range of cannon fire. But the two skiffs were nowhere in sight.

"Drop yer anchor an' hold yer position!" a sea dog shouted across the water. "Yer precious Admril—he be ar pris'ner now!"

Mr. Calico shook his fist. "We've been had!" he muttered. "Drop the anchor, mates."

"I knew it was a trap!" Charles squeaked. "The Admiral should never have agreed to go."

The whole crew of the *Nine Lives* groaned. Oliver saw the anger and frustration on their faces. What could they do now?

Again the sea dog shouted to them. "Ye'd best behave yerselves, ye cats, should ye wants ta see yer precious Admril agin!"

Mr. Calico frowned. "Where *is* the Admiral?" he called. "Where's Crag?"

"Oh, Cap'n Crag, he's takin' care of the Admril on the island," said the pirate. "But I gots his orders fer ye!"

"Orders!" snorted Charles.

Mr. Calico paced angrily up and down the deck. Finally he leaned over the ship's rail.

"Set the Admiral free!" he shouted. "We'll let you out of the bay, no harm done."

"Now wouldn't that be a pretty pichure?" The sea dog's laugh boomed through the haze. "But no deal! Now here's yer orders should ye wants ta get yer precious Admril back. Fer a ransom, ye'll give us all the booty on the *Nine Lives,* includin' all yer cannonballs. Ye've got til noon tomorrow!"

Mr. Calico turned to Charles and Oliver. "I'm sorry, mates. I should have stopped the Admiral somehow." Then he shouted his answer across the water. "Rest assured, we'll do whatever is necessary to secure the safe return of our Admiral."

Charles shook his head. "We can't let them do this," he said with a sigh. "If we give them all our ammunition, they'll have us on the run all across the Cattibean!"

"Well," said Mr. Calico. "I didn't actually say we'd pay their ransom, now did I?"

Charles's eyes brightened. "No, you didn't, Mr. Calico. So what is your plan?" Oliver leaned closer.

The first mate rubbed his whiskers thoughtfully. "Don't have one yet." He sighed.

Oliver's stomach rumbled. "All this terrible turn of events—it's making me hungry."

Mr. Calico gave him a sad smile. "You're right, my good mouse. Perhaps a little breakfast might help us to come up with a plan. We have a few coconuts in the cabin. Come along."

So the three friends sat around the Admiral's table, and Mr. Calico split open a coconut.

Oliver climbed into one half of the big nut. He slurped out the milk and gnawed at the sweet meat inside. Delicious!

But Charles didn't eat anything. He looked like he was still thinking. "If only we could have sneaked onto the island with the Admiral," he said. "Then maybe we could have set him free." He stopped for a minute. "Wish we could swim there. But it is awfully far to the beach."

"I'm not much good at swimming!" Oliver said between bites. "Besides, the sun is burning off the haze in the bay, and what if the pirates see us? We'd be cannonball targets for sure!"

Oliver glanced at the sad faces of his friends and popped into the hollowed-out coconut for another bite. When he came back up, still chewing, Charles was staring at him.

"I've got it!" he squeaked. "Actually, you've got it, Oliver!"

Mr. Calico looked puzzled, and Oliver stared at his friend.

"It's the coconut!" squeaked Charles. "Er, the cannonball! What I mean to say is—a coconut cannonball!"

Chapter Five
Just Another Coconut

Inside the big coconut-cannonball, Oliver felt himself flying over the bay. He and Charles braced themselves for a hard landing.

THUMP! Fump! Then *clumpety, clump, clump, clumpety, clump.*

It felt to Oliver as if they had been caught in an avalanche. At least he was sure they had landed somewhere onshore. He shook himself and stood up. How long had he been lying here in the dark?

"I'm alive!" he said aloud. "Charles, are you all right?"

There was no answer in the darkness. Oliver reached out a paw to his friend. "Charles, Charles! Say something!"

Charles cleared his throat. "Good evening, sir!"

"Thank goodness you're alive, too!" squealed Oliver. "Let's get this shell open and get some fresh air."

"Sounds delightful, good fellow. I could use some air," Charles said. "But what's this about a shell?"

"Charles," Oliver said, "we've got to get out of this coconut shell and rescue the Admiral from the sea dogs. It was your plan."

"Plan, what plan?" asked Charles.

Oliver paused. "You aren't kidding, are you, Charles?"

"My good fellow," said Charles. "I'm sitting here in a dark room. Then you, without proper introduction, begin telling me tales of shells and coconuts, admirals and sea dogs. Then you suggest that the whole thing is my plan. Now, who is kidding whom?"

"You really don't remember?" asked Oliver. "Not even me—Oliver?"

"Mr. Oliver, I'm afraid that not a bit of this makes any sense to me," Charles said. "Now, if you'll excuse me, I'd really like to step out for some fresh air."

He stood up and bumped his head on the top of the shell. "Ouch! Rather a low ceiling, don't you think?"

Oliver sighed. "Oh, dear me." Things couldn't get much worse.

Just then he heard footsteps. They sounded much too familiar: *Ker-thonk, ker-thonk.*

"Shhhh!" he said.

"Aargh!" snarled a voice in the distance. "If'n the Cap'n wants coconuts fer supper, why don't he gather 'em himself?"

"Caw," called a bird.

Oliver moved closer to Charles. That must be their old enemy, the cruel sea dog with a wooden leg—and his nasty parrot.

"Aw, quit yer mutterin', O'Grady," said a voice. "Ye oughter be glad ye didn't have ta stay onboard the *Seven Seas,* keepin' watch on that ship o' cats."

"Why, Big Tom, we shoulda' just blasted them cats ta smithereens. 'Specially after they fired that cannon at us," said O'Grady.

"Sometimes I thinks ya got as much wood in yer head as in yer leg," said Big Tom. "There'll be time fer that later, after we gets their booty!"

"Caw! Caw!"

"Why, looky there! Barnacle's found us a whole pile of coconuts." That was Tom again. "At least yer bird's worth his salt!"

O'Grady muttered something, but Oliver had stopped listening. Their coconut was swaying back and forth. We're in that pile of coconuts, he thought. And the sea dogs are picking some up!

"Perhaps you could help—" Charles began. Oliver quickly covered his friend's mouth with his paws.

"What'd ye say, O'Grady?" asked Big Tom.

"Nothin'."

The coconut rocked violently, and Oliver pulled Charles down against the floor. *Whoosh. Thump!* One of the sea dogs must have picked it up and dropped it into his sack.

Chapter Six
The Sea Dog's Knife

Inside their coconut, the two mice listened with all their might.

"Let's get back ta the clearin'," said a gruff voice.

The bag of coconuts bounced along, and Oliver felt as if he had been swallowed by a kangaroo. He started to feel sick. At last the coconut stopped moving. Oliver heaved a sigh of relief.

He pressed his ear against the crack inside the shell. Deep voices called back and forth, and he could hear crackling sounds. A fire?

This must be the pirates' camp, he thought. Perhaps their prisoner, Admiral Winchester, was nearby.

"Good wark, boys!" said Crag. "Jest in time fer a little supper." Something jostled their coconut, and Oliver knew that the coconuts were being taken out of the sack.

Crack! Crack! The pirates were splitting coconuts open with their knives. Then he heard slobbering sounds.

"We must get out of here," Oliver whispered to Charles. "Or they'll have mouse tidbits with their coconut supper."

He kicked at the plug at one end of their coconut. Mr. Calico had carefully sealed them inside, just in case it fell into the water. "It won't budge. Come on, Charles, lend a hand!"

He pulled at the plug with all his might, and Charles helped too. But it was no use. It was stuck tight!

"I suppose this was a part of my plan, too, eh, Mr. Oliver?" whispered Charles.

"Of course not!" squeaked Oliver. "We've got to get out of this nut—" He stopped to listen again.

"C'mere, Big Tom," growled Crag. "Why don't ye take the gag off ar precious Admril. Give 'im a bite ta eat. He'll be needin' it fer his trip up the mountain."

"Whatcha mean?" asked Tom.

"Why 'ee's goin' up ta feed the volcano tomorrow mornin'." Captain Crag laughed. "Look at his face! Ye didn't think we wuz gonna set ye free, did ye, Admril Winny-pooh?"

Admiral Winchester's voice sounded calm and brave. "As they say, sticks and stones may break my bones, but names will never hurt me!"

"Har, har, har," the pirate captain said, laughing. "Well, now, bein' thrown inta that there volcano, now that might hurt ye, mighten it, Admril?"

All the sea dogs joined in, laughing and making fun of the Admiral.

"You'll never get away with this," said the Admiral. "When the *Nine Lives* finds out I'm not with you, there'll be nothing to prevent them from waging war on you and your stolen ship."

"Aye, but thar's yer problem, Admril. They won't find out." Crag chuckled. Oliver shivered at the awful sound.

"Pip!" said Crag. "Show 'im that dummy you've been warkin' on."

Charles and Oliver heard the "Oohs" and "Aahhs" of the whole crew of sea dogs.

"Quite a likeness of the Admril hisself, Pip. Wouldn't ye say so, mates?" Crag chuckled again. "Ya see, me dear Admril, by the time yer friends on the *Nine Lives* finds out this dummy ain't you, we'll be clean escaped!"

All the sea dogs burst out laughing once more, but Oliver was thinking fast. "Charles, we've got to help the Admiral escape! If only we could get out of here! If only—"

But footsteps were coming closer and closer to the sack of coconuts. Their coconut jerked, then rose in the air. "Time for some grub," a sea dog growled. "Here's a big one."

Thwick! Oliver heard him pull out his knife.

The pirate shook the coconut and the two mice rolled around inside. Oliver felt the coconut plunk down on a rock. *He's going to split it open!* Oliver thought.

He pushed Charles up against one wall. Then he quickly backed up tight against the other wall.

THWOP! A silver blade fell past his nose.

"O'Grady!" yelled Crag. "Ye's had too many coconuts already! I wants ye ta stand guard tonight. Ye eats any more an' ye'll be too full ta stay awake!"

"Aw, Cap'n!" The knife disappeared and Oliver heard the sea dog muttering. "C'mon, Barnacle, we gots ta stand guard," he growled.

"Caw!"

The next thing Oliver heard was *Thunk!*
Their coconut jerked and bumped. It rolled
over and over, then came to a stop and split
apart. O'Grady must have kicked it out of his
way.

Oliver crouched under his half of the shell
and peered out. There was the other half,
under a bush. It moved a little. Charles must be
inside. He watched O'Grady stomp off into the
shadows, then he scuttled across to join
Charles.

"I must say, that was a close shave!" Charles
stroked his whiskers. They looked a good bit
shorter now. "Thank you, Mr. Oliver. I believe
you saved my life."

"If only we could manage to save the
Admiral's life!" said Oliver. "Let's wait here
until the sea dogs go to sleep."

Chapter Seven
That Peg-legged Pirate

The two mice didn't have to wait long. By the time the fire had died down, snores and whistles from the sea dogs filled the night air. Oliver decided that the whole camp was asleep. But what about O'Grady? He was still hobbling around the clearing, muttering to himself.

"Mr. Oliver," whispered Charles, "what's the next part of my plan?"

"You never explained it this far," said Oliver, "but I think I've got a plan myself."

"Splendid!" said Charles. "What are we to do?"

"All you need to do is to distract that peg-legged pirate for a while—"

"Consider it done, my good fellow!" said Charles. He stood up, began to wave his arms, and yelled, "YOO-HOO!"

Oliver leaped onto Charles's back, rolled him over, and clamped a paw on his mouth. "Not that way!" he whispered to his friend. "Get out in the bushes and throw a few pebbles around. When O'Grady comes over, run ahead and throw a few more. Lead him out to the beach, then toss some pebbles out over the water for a while. But whatever you do, don't let him see you!"

"Got it!" said Charles.

Soon O'Grady acted as if he heard noises in the bush. He slipped out of the clearing and into the trees. So far, the plan was working.

Oliver shook his head. "I sure hope he doesn't get caught! Now it's my turn."

He crept into the clearing. He hurried past the snoring sea dogs with their foul breath. He stole around the glowing campfire, then stopped to look around. Over there. That tree. The Admiral was tied up and gagged and very much asleep. Oliver scampered up the tree trunk and paused next to the cat's ear.

"Admiral!" he whispered. "Admiral—" Louder this time. "Admiral!!"

But the Admiral purred gently, still sound asleep. Oliver thought for a minute, then he jumped out and yanked one of the cat's long whiskers. *Sproing!*

Admiral Winchester's eyes popped open.

Oliver yanked at the gag in his mouth. "Oliver!" the cat whispered. "How on earth—"

"Shhhh. I'll have to tell you later." Oliver began chewing at the ropes that tied the Admiral to the tree.

Soon he was free. Oliver looked around the clearing. There was the dummy Pip had made—a dummy made of coconut shells, bamboo, and some scraps of cloth. In the firelight it could have passed for the Admiral himself.

"That dummy looks just like—er—kind of like you, Admiral," whispered Oliver. "Why don't you go get it and tie it to this tree?"

"Of course!" the Admiral said.

As soon as he was finished, Oliver whispered, "Come on, let's go. Follow me!"

They took a wide route around the clearing on their way to the beach. Then they watched from the shadows as O'Grady returned, muttering to himself. The pirate passed right by the Admiral-dummy tied to the tree, and he didn't give it a second look. Admiral Winchester and Oliver walked on cat's feet, quiet as a mouse, and they made it safely back to the moonlit beach.

"I'll have one of the skiffs ready for us in a minute," said the Admiral.

"I'll go find Charles," said Oliver. He scanned the sandy beach. No sign of him. Then he heard a stone plop, out over the water.

"Charles, is that you? It's me—Oliver!"

Another stone fell into the water. Oliver turned around. Still no sign of Charles. Then a pebble dropped near his feet. Someone giggled.

Oliver looked up. There was Charles, high up in a coconut tree.

"Pretty good, eh, Mr. Oliver?" Charles laughed.

"Get down here!" squealed Oliver. "We've got to get going!"

"Wait—first watch this throw." Charles wound his arm like a clock and threw a pebble far out over the water.

"Whoooooa!" Charles teetered, off-balance from the throw. Suddenly he fell headfirst into the sand below. *THUMP!*

Oliver ran over to him. "Charles! Are you all right?"

There was no answer. Charles was limp. Oliver lifted up one of his friend's eyelids and waved a paw in front of his eyes. Charles didn't even blink.

Chapter Eight
Oliver's Plan

"Admiral," called Oliver, "is the skiff ready?"

"Aye." The Admiral had just finished getting it untied.

"I'm going to need your help," said the mouse. "Charles fell out of this tree. He's out cold!"

"Oh, dear!"

"Let's just get him into the boat," said Oliver.

Gently the Admiral lifted Charles into the boat. He pushed off from land, and the three of them floated quietly into the moonlit bay. No one had noticed their escape.

After they had drifted for a while, Admiral Winchester began to row, fumbling clumsily with the oars. He splashed a little water into the skiff, right onto Charles's face.

"What, huh?" Charles shook himself.

"Charles!" squealed Oliver. "How are you feeling?"

Charles's eyes popped open. "Oliver!"

"Don't you mean Mr. Oliver?"

"Don't be silly, Oliver!" Charles said briskly. "We've got to rescue the Admiral!"

"My good mouse," said the Admiral from behind him. "I'm quite rescued, thank you!"

"Huh?" Charles turned and stared at the Admiral.

"Now, perhaps you can fill me in on how you did it," the Admiral said.

"Me?" asked Charles. "I have no idea!"

The Admiral looked puzzled and very curious.

"I'll tell both of you later," Oliver said with a smile. "And, Charles, welcome back!"

Charles looked puzzled and very curious.

"Right now you and the Admiral have got to make a decision," said Oliver. "Which ship are we going to board?"

"Why, the *Nine Lives,* of—" The Admiral stopped. He looked as if he wasn't very sure.

"But surely those pirates on the *Seven Seas* are keeping a close eye on the *Nine Lives,*" said Oliver. "Don't you think?"

"Yes, of course." The Admiral cleared his throat.

"But they're probably not watching their other side," said Oliver. "They might not notice anything that happens on the bay side, where we're coming from."

The Admiral still looked puzzled.

Oliver pointed to the big ship in the bay. "I say we take back the *Seven Seas*. We can catch 'em by surprise. That is, if you think it's a good idea."

Charles's mouth dropped open. "Uh, Oliver?"

"What's the matter, Charles?" asked Oliver. "Don't you think it will work?"

"Uh, sure," agreed Charles. "I'm all for it!"

"Good show!" said the Admiral. "Onward, to the *Seven Seas!*"

A few minutes later, the skiff drifted silently into the shadows behind the pirates' ship. The Admiral tied the skiff to the big ship, and the three friends climbed up a rope onto the *Seven Seas.* Everything was quiet onboard. One sea dog stood guard at the opposite rail. He was looking at the *Nine Lives* through a telescope.

"Watch this," whispered Oliver. He crept up the mast and began gnawing on a rope. The rope hung a sail from the crossbar above the far rail. *Snap! Thwump!* The sail fell across the sea dog guard and covered him like a blanket. Charles and Admiral Winchester rushed over and quickly tied the pirate up inside the sail. All they could hear were muffled sea dog growls.

"Good job, Oliver!" whispered his friends.

But then they heard a snore. It stopped,
then started, then stopped again. It seemed to
be coming from the hold. What sea dog was
waking up?

Quietly the mice took their positions. The Admiral went to the other end of the ship. Then Charles climbed up above in the rigging, and Oliver hid behind a pile of cannonballs next to the hold.

Soon a burly pirate stepped up the ladder from the hold with a club in his mouth. But halfway up—*BONK!*

A cannonball hit him squarely on the head. He fell back against the foot of the ladder with his eyes closed. Now the club was stuck between his teeth.

"Good show!" called the Admiral. Oliver, on top of the pile of cannonballs, took a graceful bow.

Four more sea dogs awoke at once. They burst up out of the hold, growling furiously. "It's them cats!" They glared at Admiral Winchester, who still stood at the other end of the ship.

Then they ran for him at full speed, waving knives and clubs.

The first sea dog tripped over a well-placed oar. He flew through the air and landed with his head wedged in a cannon barrel.

The other three sea dogs hopped over the oar, around the cannon, and charged toward the cat. *THUNK!* A net of the ship's rigging dropped down onto them. They kicked and growled and twisted themselves into a tangled ball. Admiral Winchester hoisted them up off the deck with a rope and pulley.

"Gotcha!" squeaked Charles from the rigging above.

Meanwhile, Oliver scurried down into the hold. He peered under all the beds and looked into the storage rooms. Then he popped back up the ladder. "That's all!" he cried. "No more sea dogs!"

The three friends gave a great cheer. Admiral Winchester puffed out his chest. "I now officially pronounce the *Seven Seas* retaken into the service of our beloved Queen!"

Oliver and Charles cheered again.

"Congratulations, Admiral!" squeaked Oliver.

"Now, Oliver," said the smiling cat, "perhaps you would be so kind as to explain how this all happened."

"Please do, Mr. Oliver!" Charles said with a laugh.

"All right." Oliver smiled as he began. "First of all, Admiral, there was the coconut, and the cannon shot—"

He stopped. A low rumbling sound boomed across the bay. It came from the island of San Fiero!

Chapter Nine
Light of Day

As dawn broke over the sea, an eerie light shone on the other side of the sky. The glow came from the volcano on San Fiero.

"We'd better signal the *Nine Lives*," said Admiral Winchester. "We may need to leave San Fiero in a hurry!"

"Right!" said Charles. "I don't think Mr. Calico will want to leave until he knows we're all safe and sound."

"And won't Captain Tabby be relieved to hear that the *Seven Seas* is retaken!" said the Admiral. "Thanks to my friend's daring plans!" He patted Oliver on the shoulder.

Oliver felt himself blush.

A booming voice shouted out over the bay. "Pirates of the *Seven Seas,* open fire on that ship o' cats!" It was Crag, and he sounded very angry.

"I believe our dear Captain Crag is calling us!" said Admiral Winchester with a smile. "How unfortunate that his pirates of the *Seven Seas* are, shall we say, fit to be tied. Ha, ha!"

"And he wants them to open fire!" Oliver began laughing, then he stopped. "Well now, why not give him a surprise?"

Again Crag bellowed orders from the beach. "I told ye ta fire, ye snoozin' excuse fer a pirate ship. FIRE!"

"Shall we?" asked Oliver.

"Why not?" said the Admiral.

So they wheeled a cannon across the deck and aimed it toward the San Fiero beach. Crag and his crew stood there, waiting.

KA-BOOOM! A cannonball splashed in the water just in front of the pirates and showered them with spray.

"Shiver me timbers," yelled Captain Crag. "Whart kinda lame-brained sea dogs be ye? I told ye to blast the *Nine Lives,* ye mangy dogs!"

KA-BOOOM! Splash! Another shot sprayed the beach. Angry sea dogs ran to hide in the trees.

Meanwhile, Oliver was lowering the pirates' *Herring Bone* flag from the mast of the *Seven Seas*. Quickly he replaced it with the correct British flag. Then he gazed up at the flag and gave a proper salute. "Welcome back to the Queen's fleet, *Seven Seas!*" he said.

A great cheer sounded from the *Nine Lives*. "They've seen the flag!" shouted Charles.

"Then let's pull up anchor and unfurl the sails!" said the Admiral. "Surely the *Nine Lives* will do the same."

"Aye, aye, Admiral!" the mice said in chorus. Charles and Oliver scampered up and down the rigging, unfurling sails all along the way.

"I'll see to it that our sea dog prisoners get a chance to join their captain," said the Admiral. So he loaded the sea dogs onto the skiff and set them adrift in the bay, still tied and gagged.

"Why, ye flea-bitten, double-crossin' cats," yelled Crag from the beach. "When I gets me paws on ye, I'll—I'll—"

A gigantic explosion rocked the island. The volcano had erupted!

Black smoke belched out of San Fiero. Red-hot rocks shot into the air like fireworks. Hissing lava melted down the sides of the volcano, burning up everything in its path.

On the beach, sea dogs scattered into the water. Some managed to get into the skiff, and others began swimming away from the island as fast as they could.

Farther out in the bay, the *Seven Seas* and the *Nine Lives* creaked and flapped as the wind caught their sails. Slowly the two ships pulled away from the exploding island.

"Can't we go any faster?" asked Oliver.

"Give the sails a minute to catch the wind," called the Admiral. He looked up. The sky above them seemed to be filled with hot, black ashes. "I just hope the sails don't catch fire!"

A few ashes, like black snowflakes, were already starting to fall. Some were landing on the sails. The largest sail had little curls of smoke rising from it.

Chapter Ten
A Proper Sail

"What'll we do?" cried Charles.

Oliver snapped his fingers. "I know!" he said. "Soda water! I saw lots of bottles down in the hold."

"I hardly think it's the right time for that!" said the Admiral.

"Oh, but it's just the right time!" cried Oliver.

"Yes!" squealed Charles. "Help us bring some bottles up and you'll see!"

The Admiral did so as quickly as he could.

"Now, if you'll shake one, sir!" said Oliver.

The curious cat shook a bottle of soda and put it down on the deck. Oliver jumped up and pried the cork off with his teeth. *Pfsheeeeeee!* Soda water sprayed straight up into the air!

"Like a little volcano!" shouted Charles.

"Now, we'd better get busy!" said Oliver.

The mice set to work like a team of firefighters. Oliver hoisted the bottles up among the masts with ropes and pulleys. Charles rode the bottles and squirted soda on the smoldering sails.

"Good show!" called Admiral Winchester. "The *Nine Lives* is already safely out of the bay. A few more minutes and we'll be safely out to sea too."

"I can hardly wait." Charles came down for another bottle. "I'm getting thirsty."

Finally the *Seven Seas* cleared the bay's entrance. In spite of a few holes burned into the sails, all the fires were out. The three friends paused for a snack of soda water and coconuts.

But their rest was interrupted by a booming voice from behind the ship. It was Crag, with his skiff full of sea dogs. "So ye leaves us out ta sea without a sail!" he bellowed. "Whar's yer sense o' fair play?"

"Fair?" said Charles. "Since when do Crag and his crew ever think about being fair?"

Admiral Winchester looked thoughtful. "Well, dropping them a sail would be the honorable thing to do."

Oliver hopped out of the coconut shell he had been eating from. "You know, the Admiral is right, Charles. Those sea dogs do need a sail."

Oliver grinned. "And I know just the thing!" He walked back to the cabin.

Charles watched him with a twinkle in his eye. "Oh yes, that would be fair, wouldn't it?"

Admiral Winchester looked puzzled.

"Here's their sail!" Oliver came back, dragging a flag behind him. He stuffed it into an empty coconut shell. "Shall we?" he asked his friends.

"With pleasure!" said the Admiral. They loaded the coconut-cannonball into the ship's largest cannon, aimed, and shot it back over the water—*BAH-ROOOOM!* The shell burst open in midair. Out floated the black flag of the *Herring Bone.*

"Now you've a proper sail!" the Admiral called back to Crag.

"Why, ye flea-bitten dandy!" yelled Crag. "I'll get ye—an' yer pesky little mice. Jest ye wait!" All the sea dogs shook their fists and growled. The big black flag floated down and covered the angry crew like a blanket.

On the *Seven Seas,* the three friends laughed until the pirates' skiff was just a speck on the horizon behind them.

Finally Admiral Winchester asked, "Now, my good Oliver, would you kindly tell us how your plan worked for my escape?"

"Yes, please do!" begged Charles.

"Well, Admiral, first there was the coconut, and the cannon shot. . . ." As the *Seven Seas* sailed into the morning sun, Oliver leaned back to tell his story for the first of many, many times.